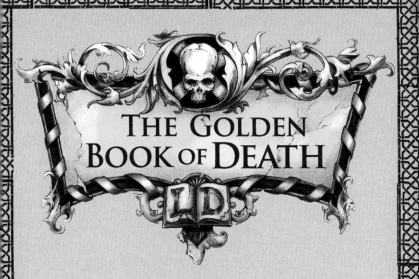

THE GOLDEN BOOK OF DEATH

BY MICHAEL DAHL

ILLUSTRATED BY SERG SOULEIMAN

Librarian Reviewer
Laurie K. Holland
Media Specialist (National Board Certified), Edina, MN
MA in Elementary Education, Minnesota State University, Mankato

Reading Consultant
Elizabeth Stedem
Educator/Consultant, Colorado Springs, CO
MA in Elementary Education, University of Denver, CO

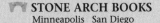

STONE ARCH BOOKS
Minneapolis   San Diego

Zone Books are published by Stone Arch Books,
151 Good Counsel Drive, P.O. Box 669,
Mankato, Minnesota 56002.
www.stonearchbooks.com

Library of Congress Cataloging-in-Publication Data
Dahl, Michael.
    The Golden Book of Death / by Michael Dahl; illustrated by
Serg Souleiman.
        p. cm. — (Zone Books — Library of Doom)
        ISBN 978-1-4342-0487-5 (library binding)
        ISBN 978-1-4342-0547-6 (paperback)
        [1. Books and reading—Fiction. 2. Librarians—Fiction.
3. Fantasy.] I. Souleiman, Serg, ill. II. Title.
PZ7.D15134Gol 2008
[Fic]—dc22   2007032226

Summary: Someone has broken into the Library of Doom! While
searching for the intruder, the Librarian is captured by a shadowy
figure—the Eraser. He has chained the Librarian to a huge golden
book. If the Librarian can't escape, all the world's books could be
could be destroyed.

Creative Director: Heather Kindseth
Senior Designer for Cover and Interior: Kay Fraser
Graphic Designer: Brann Garvey

1 2 3 4 5 6 12 11 10 09 08 07

Printed in the United States of America.

TABLE OF CONTENTS

The Library of Doom is the world's largest collection of strange and dangerous books. The Librarian's duty is to keep the books from falling into the hands of those who would use them for evil purposes.

CHAPTER 1

THE BREAK-IN!

An alarm bell is <u>ringing</u> in the Library of Doom.

Someone has **broken in!**

The Librarian stands at the window of his room.

He listens to the **bell.**

He knows where the s͟o͟u͟n͟d͟ is coming from.

The alarm is ringing in one of the **deepest corners** of the Library.

The Librarian opens the window
and **steps** **out**.

He rushes toward the ringing
alarm bell.

He must find and stop the
<u>intruder.</u>

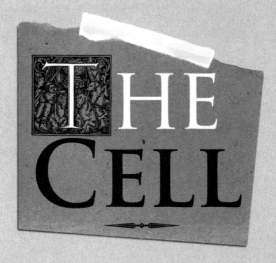

(CHAPTER 2)

THE CELL

The Librarian is the guardian of the Library of Doom.

His duty is to keep the Library's books out of evil hands.

He follows the **sound** of the ringing
bell to a room far below the Library.

The room is an **ancient**

`prison cell.`

Long ago, the room was used for locking up book thieves.

As soon as the Librarian steps into the cell, the bell stops ringing.

He hears another sound.

A metal book **flies out** of a dark corner.

The book **hits** the Librarian.

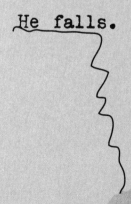

He falls.

CHAPTER 3

THE GOLDEN BOOK

When the Librarian wakes up,
he is staring at **the ceiling**.

The Librarian is **chained** to a **huge** golden book.

His wrists and ankles are held in place by **golden letters.**

A **shadowy figure** moves out of the corner. It is the Librarian's **enemy**, the Eraser.

"This cell will be your prison," says the Eraser.

"You will never again **stop** me from destroying or erasing books."

"You won't get away with this," the Librarian tells the Eraser.

"Someone will find me."

"It will be **too late**," says the Eraser.

"Too late?" asks the Librarian.
"Too late for what?"

CHAPTER 4

OVER
THE
FIRE

The golden book <u>hangs</u> from the ceiling.

Beneath the book is a fire pit.

The Eraser has filled the pit with old books.

"Old books are good for burning," says the Eraser.

Then he laughs and lights the fire pit.

The Librarian **smells** the **burning paper**.

"Nothing can help you now,"
says the Eraser.

Then he *laughs* ha ha ha ha ha ha ha and walks out
of the room.

CHAPTER 5

THE BLANK PAGE

The Librarian cannot reach any of his pockets.

They hold **special books** and tools that could help him escape.

The Librarian **struggles** against the golden letters.

It is no use. They are too **strong**.

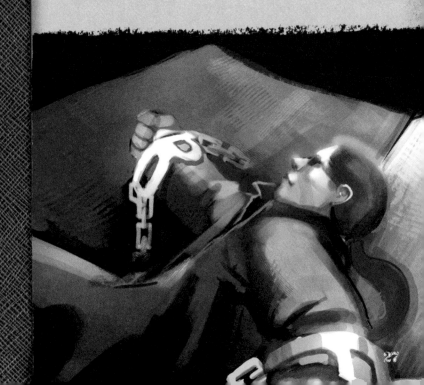

27

The golden book grows **warm**.

The Librarian can feel the **heat** against his back and legs.

Suddenly, he begins to **shake**.

A small piece of paper falls out of his sleeve.

The <u>**paper rolls**</u> into his **hand**.

Quickly, his fingers open the paper.

Nothing is written on it. The paper is `blank`.

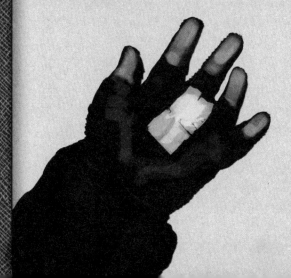

"The Eraser is right," says the Librarian to himself. "Nothing will help me now."

The blank page glows softly.

It pulls the golden letters from the (chains) onto its blank surface.

The letters form a word. FREE.

The Librarian's hands and feet
are free.

He leaps off the golden book and
puts out the fire.

"All blank pages wish to be
filled with letters," says the
Librarian.

Then he rushes out of the room,
in search of the **Eraser**.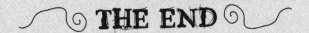

❧⟩❧ THE END ❧⟨❧

A PAGE FROM THE LIBRARY OF DOOM

GOLD

Gold has been admired for its color and its beauty ever since humans began to dig for metals in the earth. Gold was also prized for its ability to last. The shiny metal is not affected by rain, heat, or cold. Gold will not rust or tarnish either.

Gold is one of the softest metals on earth. It can easily be pounded or stretched into different sizes and shapes. One ounce of gold can be hammered into a thread that will stretch for 50 miles (80 kilometers)!

One ounce of gold can also be pounded into a thin sheet large enough to cover the floor of the average school classroom.

The deepest gold mine in the world is the **Savuka** (sah-VOO-kuh) mine in South Africa. Miners can travel more than 2 miles (3 kilometers) underground!

Gold artwork has been found in ancient Egyptian tombs over 5,000 years old.

Thin pieces of gold, known as gold leaf, are used to decorate special religious paintings known as **icons** (EYE-konz). Icons are found in Russian and Greek Orthodox churches.

Some people believe gold has magical healing powers. People drink a mixture of water and gold dust as a remedy for sickness and disease. Luckily, gold has no taste, and it will pass through the body without harming it!

ABOUT THE AUTHOR

Michael Dahl is the author of more than 100 books for children and young adults. He has twice won the AEP Distinguished Achievement Award for his nonfiction. His Finnegan Zwake mystery series was chosen by the Agatha Awards to be among the five best mystery books for children in 2002 and 2003. He collects books on poison and graveyards, and lives in a haunted house in Minneapolis, Minnesota.

ABOUT THE ILLUSTRATOR

Serg Souleiman lives and works in Carlsbad, California, as a designer and illustrator.

GLOSSARY

ancient (AYN-shuhnt)—something that is very, very old

cell (SEL)—a small room, often used for holding criminals

guardian (GAR-dee-uhn)—a person who is in charge of protecting something

intruder (in-TROOD-uhr)—someone who has broken into a place where they are not wanted

shadowy (SHAD-oh-ee)—being dark and often mysterious

thieves (THEEVZ)—people who steal things

DISCUSSION QUESTIONS

1. The Librarian is responsible for keeping the Library's books out of evil hands. What types of things are you responsible for? How do you make sure the job gets done?

2. The Librarian risks his life to protect the books inside the Library of Doom. Do you own anything that you would try to save, even if it was risky? What would you save and why?

3. This story leaves you wondering what will happen next. Do you like stories that have this type of open ending, or would you rather have the author wrap everything up? Explain your answer.

WRITING PROMPTS

1. At the end of the story, the Librarian chases after the Eraser. Pretend you are the author and write another chapter about what happens next.

2. The books inside the Library of Doom are important to the Librarian. What is the most important book to you? Describe why you like the book and why it's your favorite.

3. The Librarian says, "All blank pages wish to be filled with letters." Grab a blank sheet of paper, and write a scary story that fills the entire page with words.

INTERNET SITES

The book may be over, but the adventure is just beginning.

Do you want to read more about the subjects or ideas in this book? Want to play cool games or watch videos about the authors who write these books? Then go to **FactHound**. At *www.facthound.com*, you'll be able to do all that, and more. The FactHound website can also send you to other safe Internet sites.

Check it out!